THE BIG SNEEZE
Ruth Brown

Lothrop, Lee & Shepard Books
New York

One hot afternoon, the farmer and
his animals were dozing in the barn. The
only sound was the buzz-buzz of a lazy fly.

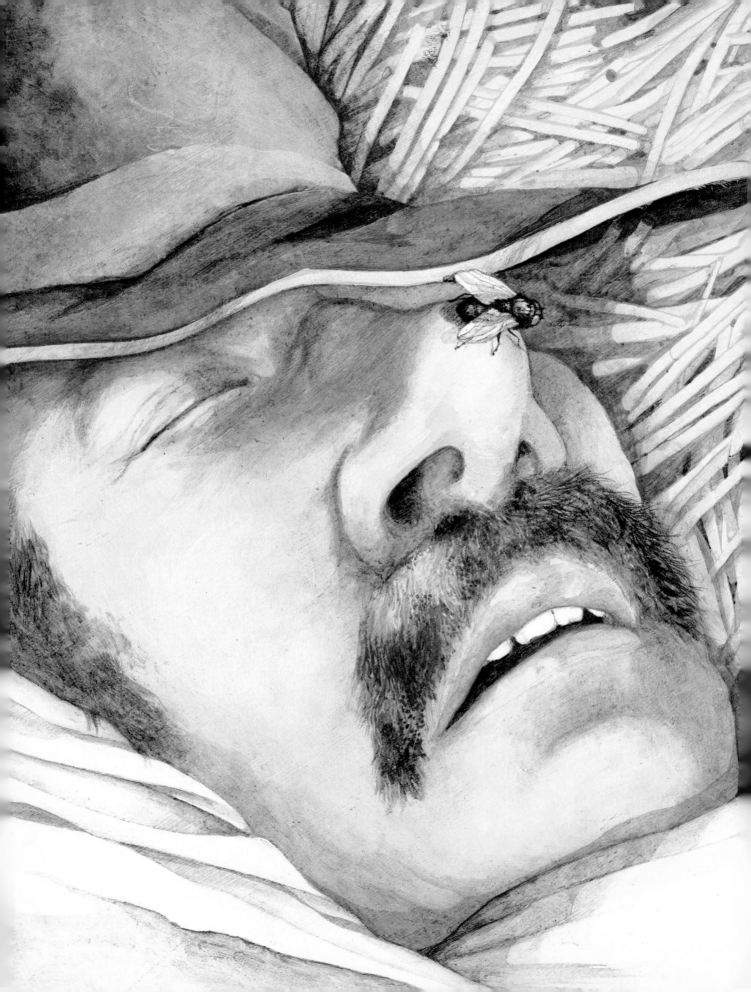

Suddenly the buzzing stopped –
the fly had landed right on the end of the farmer's nose!

"ATISHOOOOOOOOOOO!" the farmer sneezed so hard
that the fly was blown high up into a spider's web.

This disturbed the spider,
who captured the fly –

which alerted the sparrow,
who chased the spider.

This wakened the cat,
who leapt at the bird –

which woke the dog,
and frightened the rats –

who fled from the barn,
chased by the dog –

which scattered the startled
hens from their roost –

and panicked the terrified donkey!

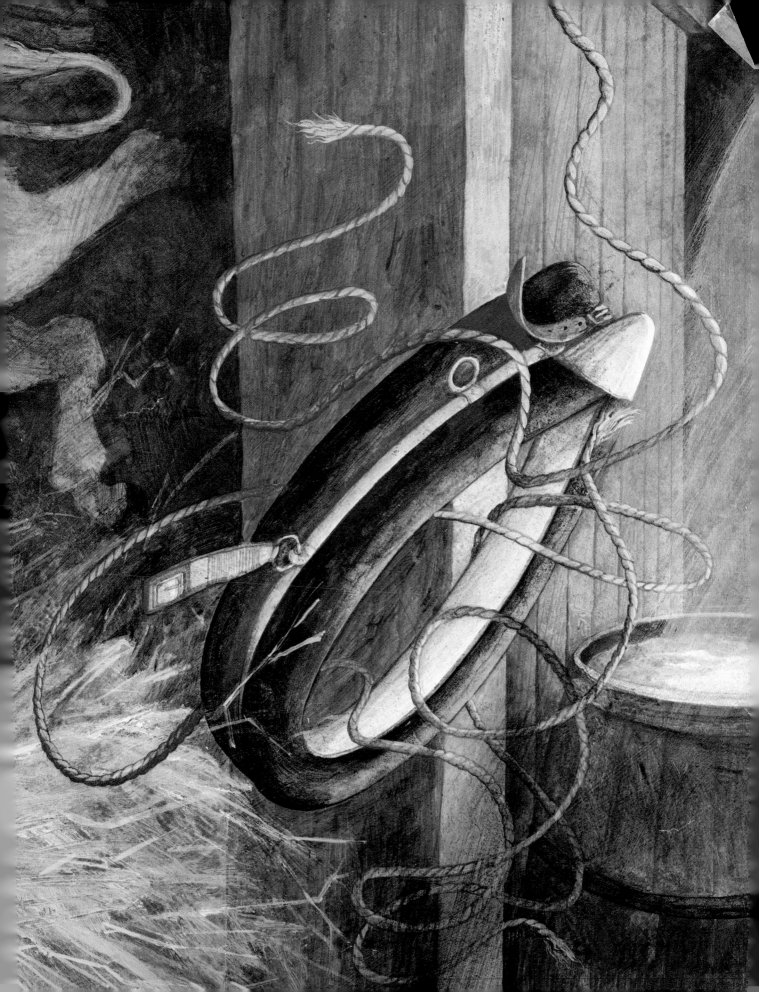

'What on earth have you done?" shrieked the farmer's wife.

"Nothing, my dear," replied the farmer. "I only sneezed!"